*For Henry Campbell Sayler*
*with love*

# Meet the

welliewishers®

The WellieWishers are a group of fun-loving girls who each have the same big, bright wish: to be a good friend. They love to play in a large and leafy backyard garden cared for by Willa's Aunt Miranda.

Willa

Ashlyn

Emerson

When the WellieWishers step into their colorful garden boots, also known as wellingtons or *wellies*, they are ready for anything—stomping in mud puddles, putting on a show, and helping friendships grow. Like you, they're learning that being kind, creative, and caring isn't always easy, but it's the best way to make friendships bloom.

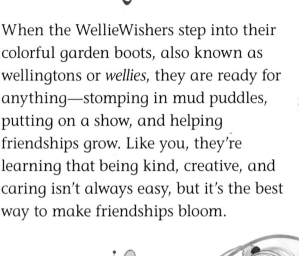

Camille

Kendall

# GARDEN MAP

Chicken Coop

Carrot's Hutch

Playhouse

Garden Gate

Aunt Miranda's House

Garden Theater Stage

Greenhouse

# Chapter 1

# Pegeen

One day, a little pink piglet was waiting for the WellieWishers at the garden gate. She had a curly tail, perky ears, and smiling eyes.

"Hello," said Kendall, kneeling down. "Who are you?"

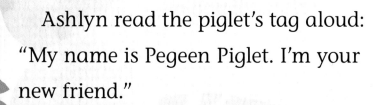

Ashlyn read the piglet's tag aloud:
"My name is Pegeen Piglet. I'm your
new friend."

"Oh, Pegeen!" said Emerson.

"You are the prettiest piglet *ever.*"

Pegeen trotted up the path ahead of the girls. Then she circled back and walked behind them, herding them forward.

"Pegeen wants us to play with her," said Camille.

"No, she wants us to follow her," said Willa, who understood animals' language. "Let's go!"

Pegeen's short legs were surprisingly fast. The girls hurried to keep up.

Pegeen led them on a winding path: past the playhouse . . .

around the pond . . .

and into the woods.

13

The girls stopped suddenly.

"*Oooh,*" they sighed, when they saw what was up ahead.

"A castle!" gushed Emerson. "Don't you just LOVE it?"

"YES!" agreed all the girls.

Pegeen sat up proudly, as if she were saying, "*This* is what I wanted you to see!"

Kendall asked, "Where did this castle come from?"

"It's from Aunt Miranda," said Willa. "Look." She held up a note.

The girls crowded around Willa to read the note. It said:

For the WellieWishers,

Thank you for filling my garden with joy every day.

Love, Aunt Miranda

P.S. Have fun with your new friend, Pegeen!

# Chapter 2

# Fairy Princesses

The girls explored the castle from top to bottom.

The castle was full of things to see, hear, taste, smell, and feel. Kendall looked at the view. Emerson listened to the bees.

Ashlyn tasted the apples. Willa smelled the flowers. And Camille felt the soft pillow.

"Let's write Aunt Miranda a thank-you note," said Ashlyn.

The girls wrote a note and left it at Aunt Miranda's door.

Dear Aunt Miranda,
We love the castle and we love Pegeen and most of all, we love YOU!

Thank you!
Xoxoxoxo

Ashlyn   Emerson   Willa

Kendall

Camille

23

The girls hurried back to the castle. "Let's pretend that we are princesses and we live in a castle," said Ashlyn.

"*Fairy* princesses!" said Emerson.
"And each one of us has a different
magical power."

25

Emerson held out her hands. "Come on, WellieWishers! You, too, Pegeen." The WellieWishers held hands.

Emerson chanted:

"*Close your eyes, stand in a row,*
*All hold hands, and off we go!*"

Princess Kendall said,
"I fill our castle with
nice things to see:

*A mirror that shines,*
*A sink like a shell,*
*Green leafy vines,*
*And two purple shelves."*

Princess Camille said, "I fill our castle with nice things to feel:
*Cushions with polka dots,*
*Breezes so soft,*
*And if you're tired,*
*A bed in the loft."*

Princess Willa said, "I fill our castle with nice things to smell:

*Daisies and tulips,*

*Gardens of blooms,*

*Green grass and hollyhocks,*

*Little mushrooms.*"

Princess Emerson said, "I fill our castle with nice things to hear:

*Humming of hummingbirds,*

*Buzzing of bees,*

*Flapping flags in the wind,*

*Rustling leaves."*

Princess Ashlyn said, "I fill our castle with nice things to taste:
*Crisp apple slices set out on plates,*
*Sweet golden honey and*
*Jam made of grapes."*

The fairy princesses were very
happy in their castle.
Until . . .

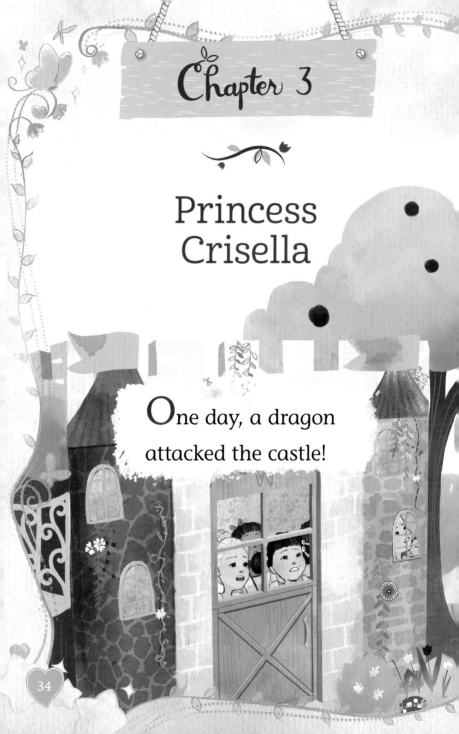

# Chapter 3

## Princess Crisella

One day, a dragon attacked the castle!

"I am Princess Crisella!" said the dragon. "I want this castle. You have to leave!"

The dragon scowled and howled. She scratched the castle walls with her sharp claws. She spewed smoke and breathed fire that burned the apples on the apple tree!

The fairy princesses tried to make the dragon go away.

We wave our wands and then we say: *Mean old dragon, fly away!*

They cast spells.

We cast spells
and chant and sing:
*Disappear, you
mean old thing!*

They wished as hard as they could.

We wish with all our fingers crossed: *Mean old dragon, you get lost!*

But their wands and spells and wishes did not work. The dragon would not leave.

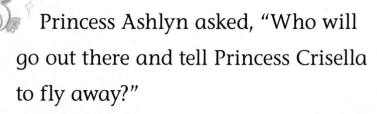

Princess Ashlyn asked, "Who will go out there and tell Princess Crisella to fly away?"

"Not me," said Princess Kendall. "She looks ferocious."

"Not me," said Princess Camille. "Her claws are sharp."

"Not me," said Princess Willa. "Her breath smells smoky."

"Not me," said Princess Emerson. "Her roar is loud."

"Not me," said Princess Ashlyn. "Her fire burns our apples. They taste like ashes."

The fairy princesses peeked at the dragon.

"You know," said Princess Camille, "when I act cranky like that, it's because something hurts."

"Same here," said Princess Emerson. "Or because no one is listening to me."

"Or I'm bored," said Princess Kendall.

"I'm cranky like that when I'm hungry," said Princess Ashlyn.

"Or I'm tired," said Princess Willa.

"But dragons don't have feelings like we do," said Princess Ashlyn.

"Maybe they do," said Princess Kendall.

"Maybe we should imagine how Princess Crisella feels," said Princess Camille.

"What for?" Princess Emerson said. "We tried to scare her away, but our magic wasn't strong enough."

"That was unfriendly, go-away magic," said Princess Willa. "Let's try a different kind of magic."

# Chapter 4

# The Magic of Kindness

Princess Willa explained her plan to the other fairy princesses.

They *loved* her idea!

They hung an invitation on the door.

Dear Princess Crisella,

Please come to tea at our castle today at 2:00.

Love from

Princess Kendall

Princess Ashlyn

Princess Willa

Princess Emerson

Princess Camille

The dragon snatched the invitation and flew off.

"Do you think Princess Crisella will come to tea?" asked Princess Ashlyn.

"If she does, I hope she won't wreck the castle!" said Princess Kendall.

"Oh, dear!" fretted Princess
Emerson. "That would be terrible!"

The fairy princesses worked all
day to prepare the castle.

Bang, bang, bang!

At two o'clock, the dragon knocked so hard that the castle door shook.

The fairy princesses shook, too!

"Here goes," said Princess Kendall. She took a deep breath and opened the door.

"Hello," she said, smiling at the dragon. "I am Princess Kendall. I fill our castle with nice things to see:

*Bubbles and butterflies,*
*Skies that are blue,*
*Princesses smiling*
*And welcoming you."*

Princess Camille led the dragon to a comfy chair.

"Please sit here," she said. "I'm Princess Camille. I fill our castle with nice things to feel:

*Toasty warm coverlets for chilly knees,*
*Cushions as velvety soft as you please.*"

Princess Willa brought the dragon a vase of flowers.

"This is for you," she said. "I'm Princess Willa. I fill our castle with nice things to smell:

*Wonderful soap that*
*Smells just like a rose,*
*Green leaves and flowers*
*To tickle your nose."*

Princess Crisella smelled the flowers and said, *"Ahhhh."*

Princess Emerson said,
"I'm Princess Emerson. I fill our
castle with nice things to hear:
*Birds that chirp sweetly,*
*Music that's slow,*
*Laughter and songs,*
*And a friendly hello!"*
Princess Emerson sang,
*"Old MacDonald*
*had a farm."*

Princess Crisella joined right in, singing in a sweet, beautiful voice,

*Ee-ii-ee-ii-oh!*

When the song ended, Princess Ashlyn handed the dragon a bowl.

"This applesauce is for you," she said. "I'm Princess Ashlyn. I fill our castle with nice things to taste:

*Cucumber sandwiches,*

*Peppermint tea,*

*Cookies, and apples*

*Picked right from our tree.*

Next time you come to tea, I will make you a delicious apple tart if you promise not to burn any more of our apples."

"I promise," said Princess Crisella, eating big spoonfuls of the sweet, tangy applesauce.

Princess Emerson played a jig on her violin, and the tea party turned into a dance party!

Princess Crisella was a good dancer, even though sometimes her tail got in the way.

# Chapter 5

## Good Friends

The dragon and the fairy princesses became very good friends. They especially liked playing in the moat of the castle. Princess Crisella's fiery breath was not a problem there.

In fact, sometimes her fiery breath was a great help. It came in handy on camping trips to start the campfire and toast marshmallows.

And the dragon was very sweet about being a comforting night-light in case any of the fairy princesses woke up in the night and felt frightened of the dark.

The dragon was terrific at popping popcorn—but sometimes she forgot to put a lid on the pan!

The fairy princesses were glad that they had decided to be kind to Princess Crisella. They were happy to have her as a friend and neighbor.

## Friendship Road Bumps

Girls love making and having friends, but the road to true friendship is not always smooth. Is your girl facing aggression or even hostility from another child? At this young age, strong emotions can flare up but usually pass just as quickly. Like the WellieWishers facing the dragon, your girl may need some help handling a friend's rough edges. Fortunately, every girl has several powerful tools in her friendship toolbox that she can rely on for such situations.

## Imagination

In much the same way that athletes imagine winning a competition, children enjoy imagining themselves overcoming their problems and achieving their goals. If your girl describes a difficult encounter with a friend, ask her to imagine a more positive outcome and then describe it to you. What would she say to her friend? How does she think the friend would react? Are there other things she could say or do that might get better results? These imagination exercises, or *visualizations,* are a natural way to practice success, for kids as well as adults.

## Empathy

When an encounter with another person is difficult or unfriendly, it can be helpful to understand why the other person acted the way they did. Empathy lets your girl put herself in another person's shoes (or wellies!) and then use her imagination to understand the other child's behavior. The WellieWishers realized that the dragon might be feeling bad—so if they could make the dragon feel better, perhaps the dragon would behave better. Once they were able to empathize with Princess Crisella, they found ways to make friends. Ask your girl why she thinks her friend acted this way. If she were in her friend's shoes, would she have acted the same way? Can she think of a way to help her friend feel and act differently?

## Patience and kindness

Remind your girl that everyone has bad days when they're not at their best—and everyone deserves another chance to do better. It would be a pity to lose a friend over one bad day or one unpleasant encounter. In the story, the dragon is unfriendly, and at first the WellieWishers just want it to go away. But by being patient and kind and giving the dragon another chance, they end up becoming great friends. Point out that often a child who is behaving badly is unhappy. Can your girl think of a way to make things better for a friend who's having a hard time? Help your girl see the value of "taking the high road" when others are not at their best. Patience and kindness usually pay off in gratitude—and an even stronger friendship.

## About the Author

VALERIE TRIPP says that she became
a writer because of the kind of person she is.
She says she's curious, and writing requires you
to be interested in everything. Talking is her
favorite sport, and writing is a way of talking
on paper. She's a daydreamer, which helps her
come up with her ideas. And she loves words.
She even loves the struggle to come up
with just the right words as she writes
and rewrites. Ms. Tripp lives in
Maryland with her husband.